UNIVERSITY AND SEX LIFE

GEORGE DAVID

ISBN: 9798839793996

CONTENTS

It was pass 3:00am and I could not sleep because I was anxious about resuming school that same day. My name is Larry Lane and I will be turning 19 in a month. I have just been admitted into the university of Lowan with my bestfriend Donald. We practically have been living our whole lives together since childhood. We are extremely close and he had come out to me first about his sexuality in sixth grade and nothing had changed since then. And now we would keep being bestfriends just like our parents had instructed that we should have each others backs and look out for one another as we have always. And we will be studying same course. Computer Engineering.

It was 7:30am already and my mom was already in my room to wake me up so I can get the day started. I was so sleepy because I couldn't sleep throughout the night so I had to wake up with sleepy eyes to prepare for the prestigious University of Lowan.

My mom and dad had decided to drop me of at the university and I ran into my bestfriend Donald. His dad's driver was there to drop him off so he sighted me and jumped out of the car to come say hello to my parents and I. We got our luggage and headed to our various dorms. We were in different dormitories but close to each other so at least we would see each other often. Got to my room and decided to arrange my stuff before heading out to eat with Donald as we planned before parting to our various dorms.

Donald and I had seen this really cool restaurant

and we would love to try it out so we got in there and browsed through the menu and then we placed our orders. I had noticed Donald and a guy close to our table making eye contacts at each other. He was black, tall about 6'3 and he was slim and a little muscular and actually very handsome. Yes, he is Donald's type and I know because he always sings it to my hearing so I just knew my friend Donald was in love already because he falls in love easily. Donald is what you will refer to as "light skinned" he is about 5'11. And I on the other hand I'm white and 5'9 and yes I am really handsome.

I guess the eye contact was a yes and he walked up to our table and asked if he could join us. I knew he was here for Donald so I let him do the talking. Donald obliged and he sat while saying thank you. He introduced his self and said his name is Leo and a first year student studying Architecture. At this point my bestfriend Donald was already having butterflies in his tummy. It was time to head back to the dorm and then Leo asked for Donald's digits and he gladly gave it to Leo. We left Leo and we headed back.

On our way back, Donald was a little silent but you could see him smile from ear to ear. Immediately I asked what he was smiling about he instantly asked me what I think of Leo and I said he seemed like a cool guy and he's handsome too…. That made Donald smile so hard. And that was when I knew my friend was in love.

CHAPTER TWO

It is the first day of class and my anxiety kicked in again. I didn't know how it would go so I hurriedly prepared and headed out. On getting to the University I saw this really cute girl. She is black and her skin was so beautiful, yeah she was beautiful and sexy too. I am not the kind of guy who lust over girls but yes I was lusting over this one here. Dirty thoughts filled my mind instantly, like how I would fuck her so bad. While I was imagining fucking this sexy ass girl boom! Donald shows up hitting my head hard.

So we headed to class.... On getting there I saw my dream girl sitting pretty. "Fuck!!!! She's so hot" I said without noticing it. Yeah Donald heard it and traced my eyes to her. He knew exactly what I was thinking so he said "Go talk to her and stop daydreaming."

Donald and I picked a sit and sat as the class was about to kick off. After class I tried walking up to her but I didn't have enough balls to do that so I let it slide. I tried again the next day to talk to her after class but I still didn't have the balls. Yes I am a virgin and had never had a girlfriend because talking to girls is actually quite hard for me. It was time to head to the dorm and I saw my crush again and this time Donald pushed me so hard to her and I just had to say something to her. "He.. Hello" and she gave me a strong glance before saying "Hi"…… I went on to tell her we were course mates and she said she knows. She went on to tell me I'm so shy and I told her "yes" with so much disappointment in my eyes. She smiled and said it was fine. Turns out we were heading same direction so we talked while walking and she said her name is Ruby. Wow Ruby I'm Larry….

"It's nice meeting you Larry. We are friends now

right?" she said.

And I said "yes... Yes... Sure" with excitement.

This girl is hot as fuck and I just knew I was going to fuck her.

Next day, I got to class and my best friend Donald was there with the hype and asking me how it went and if I fucked her... I told him to shut up and we both laughed out loud. I told Donald I would like to invite her over and he gave a nod in agreement. Boom!!... My dream girl was walking in and immediately, I waved at her and she gave me a beautiful smile... I almost melted.

After class, I walked up to her chair and this time I was bold. I asked her if she would like to come over to my dorm and she gave a little silences and I told her she can decline if she doesn't want to. I was already shaking but she agreed and said "it's fine... I will be there at 5pm". I was so happy that I almost screamed and she smiled. I told

Donald that she agreed to come and we both did our funny little dance. He said "my bestfriend is about to fuck his first pussy"

I headed to my dorm on time to clean up the room and put things in place before she arrives. I bought food and drinks and condoms just in cases she agrees.

It was 5:09pm when I heard a knock on my door. I hurriedly jumped up and went to open the door and yes it was Ruby. She's here…. What a dream. She smiled and gave me a slight hug and a big smile and I ushered her in. I offered her food and a juice and we both ate and drank. I waited for the right moment to play the porn I had downloaded on my laptop and played it. At this point I was a little scared that she might get upset but NO she wasn't. Actually, she seemed to enjoy it. And before I knew what was happening. She came on top of me and kissed me passionately and placed my hands on her medium size ass and I began to squeeze them.

She gave a slight moan…

I shifted her panties from the short gown she was wearing and fingered her with one finger... Then two fingers...

She was already dripping wet and moaning a little louder than before.

I turned her and went on top of her and she brought out my hard rocked dick and started sucking it.. It felt really good.

She kept sucking while I squeezed on her breast. They were slightly big and she sucked my dick till I came. I groaned while I came in her mouth. My dick was still hard so I knew it was time to fuck her then I brought out the pack of condom and wore one, slid my dick in her wet ass pussy.... She moaned loudly, and I kept stroking in and out. Her pussy was so wet and felt good.

We changed the style from missionary to doggy... I fucked her and her ass was clapping and jiggling.

She kept moaning and saying "Fuck me baby... yeah give me that dick... fuck me hard." I kept fucking her till she squirt all over and this time the moaning was loud and her legs were shaking profusely..... I came the second time and my dick went soft.

She freshened up and wore her cloth and told me she was ready to leave and she gave me a passionate kiss and left.

CHAPTER THREE

Friday was the next day and I was to go to Donald's dorm for the weekend but he had cancelled. He said he was going to be partying with Leo. He told me this while we walked to class and he immediately remembered that I had Ruby over. Then he went on to bug me to tell him what transpired and if I fucked her. Yes, I was going to tell him so I told him how I fucked her and how she craved my dick.... He screamed!!!... And I stopped him from screaming. Donald now knew I was no longer a virgin. He had his first gay sex last year at 18 and he said he's bottom.

We went to class and found Ruby sitting pretty as always. She immediately stood up when she saw me walking in and came to gave me a big hug...

Damn!!!!!!!!!!!

In front of the whole class.... I was shy and also very happy. We went to our seats as class was about to commence.

At Friday evening Donald had told me he was on his way to Leo's place and we should go together but I declined and told him to have fun and call me if anything goes wrong there. He nodded in agreement and said he would come to my dorm as soon as he is back the following day.

Donald came back on Saturday and seemed like he had a great time with Leo. He began narrating what happened at Leo's place. He said he got to Leo's place for the party that Friday night and there where lot of people there, loud music, food and drinks. Leo showed him around his house which was a mansion. Yeah, Leo's mom is wealthy and is always out of town for business trips .She's a single mom and extremely hard working. He showed him his room that was upstairs and that was when the mood set in. They stared deeply at each other's eyes and Leo came closer to Donald for a passionate kiss. Leo kissed and licked on Donald's neck and immediately took off Donald's shirt. Slowly kissing and licking his chest while Donald went in to grab Leo's hard cock in his brief and gently massaging his cock....

Leo moaned softly and by this time they were both naked in the room.

Leo went down to give Donald the best blowjob of his life... Sucking and licking his dick and he gradually proceeded to Donald's balls and sucked them. This made Donald moan louder..... His legs were shaking tremendously.

Donald went on to suck Leo's dick and he sucked it perfectly and it was wet... Leo was about 8 inches long and 5cm in width. His dick filled Donald's mouth and he took it all. Sucking and licking Leo's balls...

Leo moaned loudly staring deep into Donald's eyes as Donald sucked his dick while keeping eye contact with Leo.

Leo brought out a condom from his pocket and wore it on his hard dick there was a lube on the table… Seems like this was planned… He bent Donald in the doggy position and fucked him good.

Donald moaned loudly, "fuck me… fuck me… fuck me. Yeah daddy"

And Leo kept fucking his tight bussy and there was so much creampie . Donald's leg shook profusely with Leo kept fucking him hard.

When it was time for Leo to cum, he took out the condom from his dick and came on Donald's face. Groaning and moaning while he came, and fell on Donald after cuming.

They dressed up and went to downstairs to the part. Later that night Leo asked Donald to be his boyfriend and Donald agreed.

Donald was explaining the whole incident when his phone rang….

You already know who's calling… Yes, it was his boyfriend Leo. Donald picked the call with so much joy and they spoke at length.

Leo will be coming to pick Donald up for a date…. My friend is in love just like I was in love with Ruby. Maybe I should call her and take her out on a date too. I picked up my phone to call her and she picked. I asked her out on a date and she obliged. YES!!!!!

Donald had gone back to his dorm to prepare for his date with his boyfriend and I will also be preparing for a date with Ruby… I will ask her out and hopefully she agrees to be my girlfriend….

I dressed up nicely put on some cologne and went to her dorm to pick her up. I called her and told her I was downstairs and she came down in no time. She was looking beautiful as always in her gorgeous outfit it was a mini skirt and a beautiful T shirt. We went to the movies, got popcorn and drinks and the movie was about to start so we went in.

The romantic scene in the movie was so hot.

While we were watching I put my hand on her thigh and slowly proceeded to her pussy. She gave me a sexy smile and I continued. I fingered her slowly and steadily...

She moaned a little with her hand covering her mouth...

I added another finger to make it two fingers... I kept fingering her while I kissed her till her pussy became wet... She enjoyed it. The movie was over and we went to have ice cream when I popped up the question... " I love you ruby.... will you be my girlfriend?"

She stood up and ran off.....

CHAPTER FOUR

I went after her to know why she ran off and she angrily shouted at me and told she has a boyfriend and can't be my girlfriend. I shed a tear on hearing this because I mean, I was already in love with this girl for God sake. I left her there and went to my dorm. I got to my room and began to ask myself questions….

Why did she keep leading me on?

Why didn't she tell me she had a boyfriend?

Why didn't she tell me she didn't like me?

I didn't plan to fall in love with her.

I called my bestfriend Donald and I kept crying on the phone whilst I spoke to him… "Larry calm down… calm down and talk to me. Okay I'm on my way to you" he said. In no time he arrived. I cried even more when I saw him. "I'm sorry for interrupting your date Donald" I said.

"It's not a problem. What's up. What happened?" Donald said.

I explained everything to him and he drew me close and gave me a shoulder to cry on and told me to forget about Ruby that there are a lot of girls who would love me and who would do anything to be in a relationship with me. I was a little relieved but the thought of her kept flashing at me and all our sexual moments. I mean this is the girl that took my virginity.

Monday had arrived so quickly, it had been a shabby weekend for me… This was my first ever heartbreak and I must say it wasn't easy for me but I had to get up and prepare for class. I got to class that morning and found Ruby talking romantically with another guy.

Xavier, he was tall, athletic and handsome. I pretended not to notice them… Donald gave me this "don't think about shit" kind of look.

He walked to where I was seated and gave me a head rub and we did our little hand shake ... he retired to his seat.

Ruby and Xavier were still lovey dovey... But I wasn't paying attention but I was seeing everything and I must confess it really hurt!!!

She noticed my presence and became more intense with was she was doing with Xavier... Kissing and smooching him.

Class was over and I decided to go talk to her... It was stupid right? but I went anyways. She was standing with Xavier... "Hello Ruby" I said and she bluntly ignored me and went off with Xavier. I was fucking embarrassed but I kept calling her even as she kept ignoring me.

The next day at school we were given a project to work on and I was paired with Sarah. Sarah was cute but not as cute as Ruby facially but she had what Ruby didn't have in abundance and it was her mad curves. Sarah had a fat ass and massive boobs... She was curvy and sexy as well... Dark skinned and was Rich.

Sarah quickly came to me to talk about our project work and the ideas she had. Yeah she was smart and intelligent. And she asked me if I could stop by her place so we could exchange ideas. Of course I agreed to stop by. I got to my room after school and rested a little and went off to Sarah's place. On getting there I knocked on the door and she opened just in time and gave me a welcome hug as she lead me in...

She was wearing a bra top and a bum short and my eyes went straight to her fat ass... the short wasn't covering her fat ass completely and I instantly go a semi hard dick. She noticed this while I was seated and smiled sexily. "ehm so what ideas should we go with" I said in confusion and she brought out her computer and presented me with what she had put together.

"Impressive" I said and she thanked me and added a sexy smile to it. "I don't think we need to add anything else because this is perfect" I said while I made eye contact with her massive boobs that hung standing on her chest. She traced my eyes and took the computer away from me and instantly planted a kiss on my lip. I was shocked but yeah I wasn't going to stop for anything. So I kissed her back and it started there...

She quickly unzipped my pant and brought out my hard dick and kept massaging it. Suddenly, she started sucking my dick... spat on it and sucked my dick hard...

I moaned, and she kept sucking. She sucks very good...

"Damn!!! Yeah suck my dick baby"... Hmm keep sucking..

She came on top of me and rode my dick so madly... this made me moan aloud... She gave a slight moan while she was riding my hard dick. I grabbed her massive boobs and squeezed them on my face and sucked those tits like my life depended on it. Now she was moaning loudly...

Also went to grab her fat as while I spanked them a little… Yeah she loves it.

She kept riding till I was about to cum… "I'm cuming… I'm cuming" I moaned aloud.

She kept on riding and this time intensely. Her fat ass was clapping against my thighs…Her pussy was so wet and I could feel it dripping wet… I took out my dick and came all over her body. She gave me a satisfied smile and I responded, wore my pants and told her I would see her at school tomorrow.

7:00am the next morning I woke up, had breakfast, dressed up and headed out. On getting to class I saw Ruby and her boyfriend Xavier doing the same thing they were doing the other day and this time I wasn't even interested in her anymore. I had already moved on already.

Sarah came to say hello to me and to handover the project work to me because she wanted me to keep it. While we were talking I could notice Ruby stare at us in disgust but I didn't pay no minds.

Sarah and I became really close and attached to each other. I always enjoyed her company. Donald also likes her and told me to ask her out but I was scared because I didn't want what happened between I and Ruby to happen with Sarah. I was willing to settle with what Sarah wanted but honestly, I didn't know what she wanted and at the same time I didn't want to mess things up.

Donald had told me to try and maybe do it over the phone. I obliged and picked up my phone and texted her, she responded almost immediately. And I asked her to be my girlfriend and she agreed.

She agreed!!!!!! I told Donald about it. He was extremely excited for me.

Went over to Donald's place to chill and I meet Leo over there. We exchanged pleasantries. Larry will you mind coming to my place... I'm holding a party on Friday night and I want to invite you" Leo said.

Donald kept pushing me to say yes so I wasn't

going to decline…

"I'll be there" I said with a little smile.

CHAPTER FIVE

At 8:00pm on that Friday, my bestfriend Donald was already at my room and we left for Leo's party. We arrived at the party and all I could say was WOW. Leo indeed lives in a big mansion and it looked beautiful. The music was buzzing loudly with so much people in the room, drinking and smoking, two guys making out at a corner in the room, a guy fingering a girl. "Oh you guys are here already" Leo said while walking up to us immediately he sighted us.

He kissed Donald a welcome kiss and shook my hands...

He poured us a drink and told us to enjoy the party... 5 minutes later Leo came to take Donald to the dance fall. I was sitting there while sipping my vodka suddenly a pretty girl walked up to me and asked if I was here alone I said "no I'm here with my friend" while pointing to the direction Donald and Leo were dancing and YES I couldn't find them there anymore. They were probably fucking already.

I told her to excuse me and I would be back shortly. I stood up and went in search of Donald. I searched all the rooms upstairs...

When I wanted to open the last room, I heard loud moans... Yeah right!! I could hear Donald and Leo moaning aggressively. All I could hear was "Fuck me Leo yeah!!!! Right there baby"... "You nasty hoe, Donald" I said with a smile... I was a little turned on anyways.

Went back to the pretty girl downstairs and we got talking. She said her name was Chloe. Nice name I said while she was acting all sexy.

It felt like a dream when she asked me if I was interested in having a threesome. I freaked out a bit but on the other I was dying to try it so I told her "Okay… where is the third person"…. She signaled a guy to come. A guy?!! I was really hoping it would be a girl though but I didn't say anything about it to her. The guy came to us and he kissed Chloe on the lip. She introduced him as her boyfriend. Okay at this point I was surprised but I didn't show it… He said his name was Mack. We shook hands and signaled me to follow her and we all went upstairs to a room.

We got in the room and Chloe started to undress…

She was already naked… Mack also was…

And they told me to undress and I did. Mack and Chloe started kissing and they pulled me to join in…

Chloe kissed me while Mack gave her head. Chloe went down to dive Mack a blowjob. It started getting interesting when Mack started kissing me. At first I didn't enjoy it but later it started to feel good. It turns out Mack is bisexual…

Mack began to fuck Chloe while she sucked my

hard rock dick...

My dick in her mouth didn't make her loud moans too audible... Mack signaled me to come fuck Chloe... I fucked her in doggy style while she sucked Mack's 9 inches dick. We switched the position to missionary and I fucked her while sucking her boobs... Her nipples were big and hard... I teased one nipple with my hand while Mack sucked the other.

Mack began to wank his dick which turned me on. I never thought it would but it did. This was me fucking a girl and watching another guy wank.

We were about to cum and Mack came on Chloe's face while I came on her wet pussy. It felt really good. We cleaned up and I first left the room first. I came out of the room and say Donald searching for me. "Where have you been" he said. "I was around. Where have you been?... I searched for you and found you. I didn't want to distract you and Leo" I replied with a teasing smile on my face. He laughed out loud with a slight cough.

The party was over and we headed back to my dorm. As soon as we got to my room we blacked out completely.

Monday morning, I woke up and prepared for class. Got to school my Donald was already in class and exchanged pleasantries and my girlfriend Sarah, walked up to me with a warm kiss and warm embrace.

At this point Ruby saw this and you could tell she was jealous but I was already over her and didn't want anything to do with her.

Class was over and I needed to visit the library for a homework and I met Ruby on the way... she tried talking to me to ask for forgiveness and told me she loves me and I told her I was already in love with Sarah.

Ruby went on to convince me to date her and break up with Sarah and obviously I turned her down. She told me she broke up with Xavier because he cheated constantly and would always hit her if she tried to complain about his cheating act. And she tried to kiss me but I pulled myself off and took my leave. Ruby kept calling my name "Larry!!! Larry!!!" but I didn't look back as I kept on walking. She cried…. I was touched but I didn't want to make another mistake.

Exams were fast approaching and I didn't want any distractions. Donald Sarah and started to work really hard, we studied hard and attended classes regularly.

CHAPTER SIX

My birthday was the next day and I didn't plan on doing anything because I'm not really someone who actually likes to celebrate birthdays.

The next day… That morning I was still in bed sleeping when I heard a loud "Happy birthday!!!!" I quickly jumped up and I was surprised when I say Donald, Sarah and Leo. How did they get in? Oh Donald has my spare key.

I gave Sarah a kiss as she handed me a gift. They brought a cake with 19 candles on it. I was actually happy to see them… I was filled with joy as I smiled from ear to ear and they sang happy birthday to me and handed the cake to me… I made a wish and blew the candles and then we headed to school together.

They waited for me while I went to shower and we headed to class together.

After class I decided to treat Donald, Sarah and Leo to lunch and they were happy about it. We went to a really good restaurant and we enjoyed our meals and made a toast to more years.

Fast forward to exam week...

My bestfriend Donald, my girlfriend Sarah and I have been preparing so hard for our exams. We are actually brilliant student despite our sex lives. We worked extremely hard for our grades. And Sarah, very helpful despite her huge sex drive she's smart.

We wrote our exams and came out tops. We continued like that and now we are in our final year of school and our grades has been outstanding.

My love grew stronger for Sarah and we loved

each other deeply and would do anything to stay together. There where ups and downs but we let love lead.

Donald and Leo were still together waxing stronger and I'm so happy for them especially my friend Donald because he got his heart broken a lot before university but I'm glad he finally found the right person for him.

I had gone home a couple of times with Sarah and she met my parents and they really do like her. Also went to her house and met her parents and they were nice to me.

On our graduation day my parents and Donald's parent came as well. Our parents were so happy.... What made them happy the most was the fact that we graduated with a first class. This was only possible because of the amount of hard work we had put into it and it was worth it.

Leo walked up to us standing with our parents and Donald went on and held Leo's hand and introduced Leo as his boyfriend to his parent and yes they accepted him and blessed them.

We had an after-party that night we changed our outfits to something more club like and went on to party all night.

THE   **END**